To Mom and Dad—for Tahoe summers, nature hikes, and wildflower bouquets. For finding immeasurable joy in life's small moments.
—Karen

To all wildlife.
—Marc

Library of Congress Cataloging-in-Publication Data available.

ISBN 978-1-4521-7063-3

Manufactured in China.

Design by Amelia Mack.
Typeset in Goldenbook.

10 9 8 7 6 5 4 3

Chronicle Books LLC
680 Second Street
San Francisco, California 94107
www.chroniclekids.com

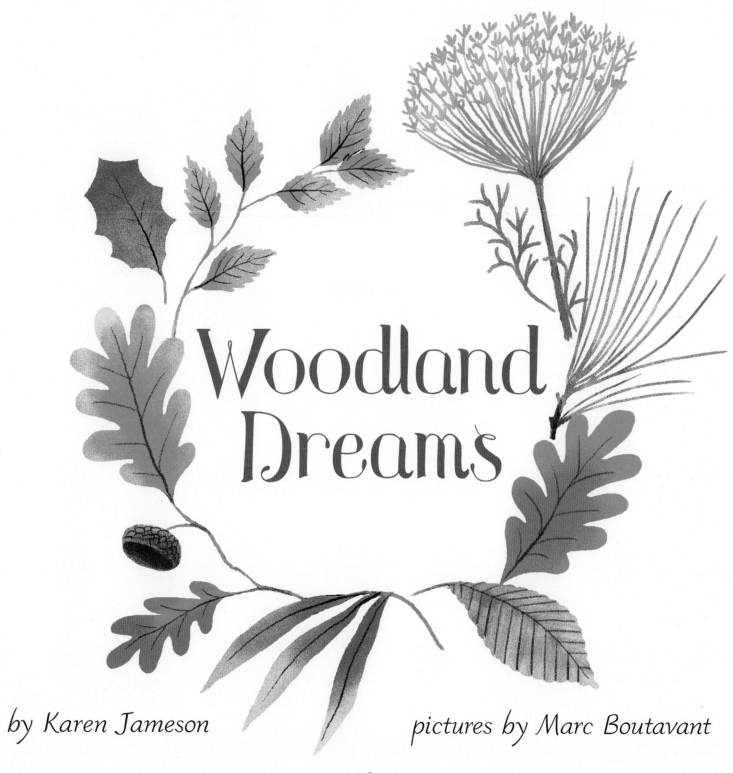

Woodland Dreams

by Karen Jameson

pictures by Marc Boutavant

chronicle books · san francisco

Come home, *Big Paws*.

Berry picker
Honey trickster
Shadows deepen in the glen.
Lumber back inside your den.

Come home, *Velvet Nose.*

Antlered swimmer
Pond-weed skimmer
Daylight's fleeting—wade ashore.
Bed down in the great outdoors.

Come home, *Tiny Hooves*.

Wide-eyed runner
Spotted sunner
Evening's sounding. Scurry! Rush.
Safely nap in wooded brush.

Come home, *Swift Legs*.

Furry schemer
Red-tailed dreamer
Night wind's blowing. Trot this way.
Mountain den's your hideaway.

Come home, *Long Ears.*

Meadow hopper
Clover cropper
Twilight whispers. Time to furrow.
Curl up tight inside your burrow.

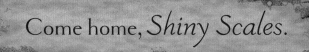

Come home, *Shiny Scales*.

Wild-tail splasher
Cascade crasher
Air's cooling close to shore.
Slow to rest on water's floor.

Come home, *Hard Shell.*

Midday napper
Sudden snapper
Dusk's upon us. Almost home.
Pull inside your comfy dome.

Come home, *Strong Beak.*

Woodland borer
Bug adorer
Darkness beckons. Take to flight.
Snooze in tree hole overnight.

Come home, *Bushy Tail.*

Tree-top dasher
Acorn stasher
Moon is rising. Scamper. Climb.
Doze in nook 'til morning time.

Come home, *Painted Wings*.

Nectar sipper
Dizzy dipper
Stars are twinkling. Flutter. Search.
Light upon your leafy perch.

This way, *Small Boots*.

Brave trailblazer
Bright stargazer
Cabin's toasty. Blanket's soft.
Snuggle deep in sleeping loft.

Every creature's tucked in tight.
Woodland dreams swirl 'round tonight.